To Kill a Mockingbird

Lightbox Literature Studies

Piper Whelan

LIGHTB◆X
openlightbox.com

LIGHTBOX

Go to
www.openlightbox.com
and enter this book's
unique code.

ACCESS CODE

L B H 8 3 9 4 6

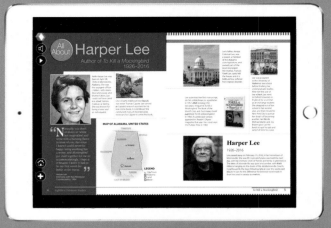

Lightbox is an all-inclusive digital solution for the teaching and learning of curriculum topics in an original, groundbreaking way. Lightbox is based on National Curriculum Standards.

STANDARD FEATURES OF LIGHTBOX

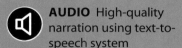 **AUDIO** High-quality narration using text-to-speech system

 WEBLINKS Curated links to external, child-safe resources

 INTERACTIVE MAPS Interactive maps and aerial satellite imagery

 VIDEOS Embedded high-definition video clips

 SLIDESHOWS Pictorial overviews of key concepts

QUIZZES Ten multiple choice questions that are automatically graded and emailed for teacher assessment

 ACTIVITIES Printable PDFs that can be emailed and graded

 TRANSPARENCIES Step-by-step layering of maps, diagrams, charts, and timelines

 KEY WORDS Matching key concepts to their definitions

 MORE Extra information and details on the subject

 FIRST HAND Letters, diaries, and other primary sources

 DOCS Speeches, newspaper articles, and other historical documents

Contents

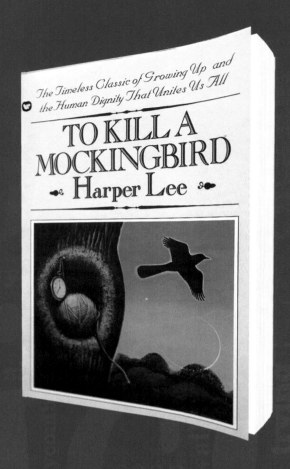

Analyzing a Newspaper Article

Students will assess a newspaper article and write an analysis. An exemplary analysis will meet the following criteria.

- Identifies the topic of the article
- Identifies the main points and opinions presented in the article
- Identifies the writer of the article
- Presents information about the writer and infers how his or her life may have shaped this opinion
- Assesses the writer's reliability
- Analyzes how the writer makes his or her argument
- Uses evidence from the article to show how the writer supports his or her argument
- Analyzes the writer's use of literary devices to enhance the article
- Differentiates between the facts and opinions presented in the article
- Identifies when and where the article was published, and determines its intended audience
- Identifies and understands the goals of the article
- Assesses the effectiveness of the format (a newspaper opinion article) in presenting the writer's argument
- Connects the article to the societal and historical context in which it was written
- Infers what is not said about this topic in the article
- Identifies what information is unintentionally implied in the article
- Infers what other opinions may be presented about this topic and who may be most likely to express them
- Uses a number of other resources to analyze the context of the article

All About Harper Lee
Author of *To Kill a Mockingbird*
1926–2016

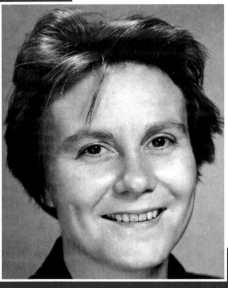

Nelle Harper Lee was born on April 28, 1926, in Monroeville, Alabama. She was the youngest of four children, with sisters Alice and Louise, and brother Edwin. Lee could not have cared less about fashion, makeup, or dating. She was known for being a loner and an individualist.

One of Lee's childhood best friends was writer Truman Capote. Lee served as Capote's research assistant for his true-crime book, *In Cold Blood*. She conducted many of the interviews necessary for Capote to write this book.

"Naturally, you don't sit down in 'white hot inspiration' and write with a burning flame in front of you. But since I knew I could never be happy being anything but a writer, and *Mockingbird* put itself together for me so accommodatingly, I kept at it because I knew it had to be my first novel, for better or for worse."

Harper Lee
Interview with Roy Newquist
Counterpoints, 1964

MAP OF ALABAMA, UNITED STATES

TENNESSEE

GEORGIA

ALABAMA

● Birmingham

MISSISSIPPI

● Montgomery

☆ Monroeville

FLORIDA

GULF OF MEXICO

LEGEND
● City/Town
□ Alabama
□ Land
□ Water
☆ Featured Place

Lee's father, Amasa Coleman Lee, was a lawyer, a member of the Alabama state legislature, and owned part of the local newspaper. Her mother, Frances Finch Lee, rarely left the house, and it is believed she suffered from bipolar disorder.

Lee was accepted to the University of Alabama's law school before finishing her undergraduate studies. After her first year of law school, Lee went to Oxford University in England, for a summer as an exchange student. She dropped out of law school in her second year, and then moved to New York City to pursue her dream of becoming a writer. Her friends Michael Martin and Joy Brown gave Lee the funds to quit her job and write full time for a year.

Lee submitted her first manuscript, *Go Set a Watchman*, to a publisher in 1957. After revising it for two years, it became *To Kill a Mockingbird*. The Book of the Month Club and the Literary Guild published *To Kill a Mockingbird* in 1960. A condensed version appeared in *Reader's Digest* magazine that year. Her novel won the Pulitzer Prize in 1960.

 Google Maps

Monroe County Heritage Museum, Monroeville, Alabama
Explore Harper Lee's hometown using the street view of the former Monroe County Courthouse, now a museum with an exhibit dedicated to her.

Document

Harper Lee Was My David Bowie: How '*Mockingbird*' Changed One Writer's Life
Cite specific evidence in Margaret Stohl's newspaper article on how *To Kill a Mockingbird* affected her as a young adult author.

1. Margaret Stohl writes that in *To Kill a Mockingbird*, Harper Lee gives young readers a "sense of choice, of agency." How does Lee achieve that? Use specific examples from the novel.
1. Stohl calls this novel "the most important book of my life." What do you consider the most important book in your life? Why? What does it mean to you?

First Hand

Notable People Pay Tribute to Harper Lee
Compare and contrast the three perspectives provided in these quotations about Harper Lee's life and legacy.

1. What is similar about these three perspectives? Where do they differ?
2. After analyzing these perspectives, what can you infer about Harper Lee as a writer and as a person?

Harper Lee

1926–2016

Lee passed away on February 19, 2016, in her hometown of Monroeville. She was 89. A private funeral was held the next day, with her intimate circle of friends and family in attendance. The town of Monroeville was quiet and somber, with black ribbons hanging on the doors of the old Monroeville County Courthouse. In the days following, fans all over the world paid tribute to Lee for the difference her beloved novel made in their lives and in society as a whole.

Researching for a Writing Assignment

Students will complete a thorough research process to prepare for a writing assignment, and organize their research in a logical manner that supports their writing. An exemplary research process will meet the following criteria.

- Creates a goal for the research, based on the topic and working thesis
- Creates specific, thoughtful, and inventive research questions that are relevant to the topic of the writing assignment
- Produces a list of categories, key words, and related ideas to effectively assist in researching
- Uses high-quality sources that pertain to the topic and come in a variety of formats, such as books, journals, primary sources, websites, and databases
- Determines accuracy of all sources
- Uses sources that provide balanced research and various perspectives on the topic in question
- Takes notes to highlight the key facts and ideas in order to answer all research questions
- Extracts relevant, detailed information from the sources during the note-taking process
- Organizes the research notes in a clear and concise manner
- Organizes the research notes logically and in a way that sets up the information and ideas for analysis and the writing process
- Analyzes the information and produces ideas and points to support the working thesis
- Uses an effective and suitable format to present all research
- Properly cites all sources used

Setting of the Novel

Monroeville is located in southern Alabama, between the cities of Montgomery and Mobile. Harper Lee spent most of her life in Monroeville, dividing her time between her hometown and New York City for a number of years. Many believe Lee patterned Maycomb, the fictional town in *To Kill a Mockingbird*, after the town of Monroeville. The places she knew and people she grew up with are thought to have inspired the places, characters, and way of life presented in her novel.

Snapshot

Monroeville in 1930
Total Population 2,382

Population by Ethnicity

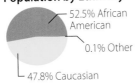

- 52.5% African American
- 0.1% Other
- 47.8% Caucasian

Education by Age Demographic

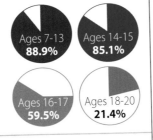

Ages 7-13 **88.9%**
Ages 14-15 **85.1%**
Ages 16-17 **59.5%**
Ages 18-20 **21.4%**

Illiteracy Rate by Ethnicity
*percentage over age of 10

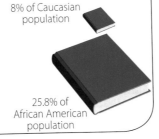

8% of Caucasian population

25.8% of African American population

The Fictional Town: Maycomb

"Maycomb was an old town, but it was a tired old town when I first knew it. In rainy weather the streets turned to red slop; grass grew on the sidewalks, the courthouse sagged in the square. Somehow, it was hotter then: a black dog suffered on a summer's day; bony mules hitched to Hoover carts flicked flies in the sweltering shade of the live oaks on the square. Men's stiff collars wilted by nine in the morning. Ladies bathed before noon, after their three-o'clock naps, and by nightfall were like soft teacakes with frostings of sweat and sweet talcum.

People moved slowly then. They ambled across the square, shuffled in and out of stores around it, took their time about everything. A day was twenty-four hours long but seemed longer. There was no hurry, for there was nowhere to go, nothing to buy and no money to buy it with, nothing to see outside the boundaries of Maycomb County. But it was a time of vague optimism for some of the people: Maycomb County had recently been told that it had nothing to fear but fear itself."

Scout Finch, Chapter 1

The 1962 film adaptation of *To Kill a Mockingbird* portrayed life in the South during the 1930s with carefully-made sets, from the Finches' quiet neighborhood to the simple, neatly kept town square and stately courthouse. The ramshackle house in the country that Tom Robinson, an African American, and his family call home stands in stark contrast to the houses in the town of Maycomb.

▶ **Video**

An Interview with Gregory Peck
Determine two or more ways that the novel's setting helped Gregory Peck to play Atticus Finch in the film.

1. Why do you think Harper Lee set the novel in a small town? What are the advantages of basing a story like this in a small town instead of a big city?

🌐 **Weblink**
Monroe County's Old Courthouse Museum
Explore the Monroe County Heritage Museum's Old Courthouse Museum webpage.

1. Imagine you are writing a novel based on your hometown and the places that shaped your childhood. What would you like the reader to understand about these places? What aspects would you like to focus on?
2. Explain why you think the Monroe County Heritage Museum decided to preserve the courtroom as it was in the 1930s.
3. Why do you think the set designers for the film adaptation of *To Kill a Mockingbird* decided to recreate Monroeville's old courtroom?

The Monroe County Courthouse was Harper Lee's inspiration for the courtroom in *To Kill a Mockingbird*. Lee would sit in the balcony as a child and watch her father practice law. The courtroom was carefully recreated for the set of the 1962 film adaptation of the novel. The courthouse now houses the Monroe County Heritage Museum.

Analyzing Famous Speeches as Arguments

Students will analyze a well-known speech as an argument and write a response. An exemplary analysis will meet the following criteria.

- Presents a strong thesis that is based on analysis of the argument presented in the speech and how the argument is presented
- Consistently uses strong textual evidence to support the thesis
- Presents an engaging and effective introduction, body, and conclusion
- Structures the analysis in a logical order
- Develops a thorough analysis of the speech
- Uses clear prose to present the student's voice and perspective
- Identifies the main points presented in the speech
- Identifies the speaker and infers how his or her life may have shaped this argument
- Identifies when and where the speech was given
- Determines the speech's intended audience
- Analyzes how the speaker makes his or her argument
- Uses strong evidence from the speech to show how the speaker supports his or her argument
- Analyzes the language used to convey the speech's argument
- Demonstrates understanding of the historical and societal context in which the speech was given and connects that context to the speaker's argument
- Properly integrates quotations
- Properly cites all sources used

Time Period of the Novel

Although Harper Lee published *To Kill a Mockingbird* in 1960, the novel is set in the early 1930s, the decade in which Lee grew up. This era is remembered for the Great Depression. This was a time when work was scarce and many people lost everything they owned. This excerpt depicts how the people who were most affected by the Great Depression struggled to survive.

Throughout the Great Depression, unemployed people lined up to eat at soup kitchens in hopes of getting their next meal for a low price.

The Great Depression

"One morning Jem and I found a load of stovewood in the back yard. Later, a sack of hickory nuts appeared on the back steps. With Christmas came a crate of smilax and holly. That spring when we found a croker-sack full of turnip greens, Atticus said Mr. Cunningham had more than paid him.

'Why does he pay you like that?' I asked.

'Because that's the only way he can pay me. He has no money.'

'Are we poor, Atticus?'

Atticus nodded. 'We are indeed.'

Jem's nose wrinkled. 'Are we as poor as the Cunninghams?'

'Not exactly. The Cunninghams are country folks, farmers, and the crash hit them hardest.'

Atticus said professional people were poor because the farmers were poor. As Maycomb County was farm country, nickels and dimes were hard to come by for doctors and dentists and lawyers."

Scout Finch, Chapter 2

President Franklin D. Roosevelt talked about the Great Depression in his first inaugural address. He urged Americans to stay strong when facing the hardships that characterized this era, such as unemployment and drought, and to not be afraid of the future.

The 1930s was also a time of racial **segregation**, with laws preventing African Americans from enjoying the same rights and freedoms as Americans of European descent. Some public places had separate spaces to keep African Americans apart from Caucasian citizens. Discrimination against African Americans was legitimized by the "Jim Crow" laws, which were first enacted after the Civil War and continued into the era in which *To Kill a Mockingbird* is set.

The trial at the center of *To Kill a Mockingbird* is thought to be inspired by the Scottsboro Trials of 1931. This was a noteworthy case in which nine African American men were falsely accused of attacking two Caucasian women in Alabama.

Analyzing a Video

Students will watch and assess a video related to a component of the novel, and write an analysis of the video. An exemplary video analysis will meet the following criteria.

- Identifies the purpose of the video
- Identifies the intended audience of the video
- Describes how the content of the video is presented
- Summarizes the information and opinions presented in the video
- Analyzes the quality of the content presented in the video
- Assesses the effectiveness of the video
- Discusses the technical aspects of the video and whether or not these enhance the content
- Determines whether the images and graphics used in the video relate to the content
- Determines whether the video is easy to follow and understand
- Gives the analysis a clear and consistent purpose
- Organizes the analysis in a logical, effective manner
- Presents a strong, clear argument about the video
- Provides strong and accurate details to support the argument about the video
- Considers other perspectives on the purpose and effectiveness of the video
- Makes connections between the video and the novel
- Properly integrates quotations from the video
- Cites all sources used in the analysis

Conflict in the Novel

In literature, conflict is a struggle between two or more opposing forces, creating a tension that must be resolved. This is the main challenge that the protagonist faces throughout the story. This struggle is often between the protagonist and antagonist, but there are other types of conflict found in literature. Conflict is a vital element in any piece of fiction. Without it, there is no story.

The Four Major Types of Conflict in Literature

MAN vs. MAN

MAN vs. SELF

The protagonist struggles against an opposing character, usually the antagonist. This is a common type of conflict in fiction, and generally features the fight between good and evil. In *Harry Potter and the Sorcerer's Stone*, Harry tries to stop Voldemort, the dark wizard who killed his parents, from stealing the Sorcerer's Stone.

The protagonist fights an inner battle with himself or herself. The battle is often about a major decision he or she has to make. His or her internal issue then affects his or her actions and motivations. In *Hamlet*, Hamlet struggles to decide whether or not to avenge his father's murder by killing his uncle Claudius.

MAN vs. SOCIETY

MAN vs. NATURE

The protagonist is opposed to the principles or actions of his or her community or society as a whole. This conflict is based upon the protagonist's beliefs or morals. In *The Hunger Games* series, Katniss Everdeen volunteers to take her sister's place in the Hunger Games. After winning, she stands up to the tyrannical Capitol, which oppresses the districts of Panem and holds the Games each year.

The protagonist faces an obstacle in nature. This may be an entire landscape or a symbolic representation of nature, such as an animal or natural disaster. In *Life of Pi*, Pi survives a shipwreck that kills his family. Stranded on a lifeboat with a Bengal tiger, he is then faced with the struggle of surviving in the middle of the Pacific Ocean with his fearsome companion.

Types of Conflict in *To Kill a Mockingbird*

The two main types of conflict in *To Kill a Mockingbird* are man versus society and man versus man. Both of these conflicts drive the major events of the story.

Man versus Society

"The witnesses for the state, with the exception of the sheriff of Maycomb County, have presented themselves to you gentlemen, to this court, in the cynical confidence that their testimony would not be doubted, confident that you gentlemen would go along with them on the assumption—the evil assumption—that all Negroes lie, that all Negroes are basically immoral beings, that all Negro men are not to be trusted around our women, an assumption one associates with minds of their caliber. Which, gentlemen, we know is in itself a lie as black as Tom Robinson's skin, a lie I do not have to point out to you."

Atticus Finch, Chapter 20

Atticus   **Society**

Man versus Man

"According to Miss Stephanie Crawford, however, Atticus was leaving the post office when Mr. Ewell approaches him, cursed him, spat on him, and threatened to kill him […] Miss Stephanie said Atticus didn't bat an eye, just took out his handkerchief and wiped his face and stood there and let Mr. Ewell call him names wild horses could not bring her to repeat."

Scout Finch, Chapter 23

Atticus   **Bob Ewell**

TEACHER NOTES

🌐 More

The Two Types of Conflict in *To Kill a Mockingbird*
Read these descriptions of conflict in the novel, and cite strong and thorough textual evidence to support analysis of the types of conflict in the novel.

1. How do the conflicts faced by characters in *To Kill a Mockingbird* change their perspectives and behavior?
2. How do the conflicts in *To Kill a Mockingbird* relate to the novel's themes?

▶ Video

Performance of "The Night at the Courthouse Steps"
Analyze how conflict is presented in this scene from a stage production of the novel.

1. Does this interpretation of the scene at the courthouse steps match the way you pictured the scene while reading it? If not, what was different?
2. In the stage adaptation of the novel, an actress playing the role of an adult Jean Louise Finch narrates the story. Explain why the playwright who adapted the novel chose to have a narrator as part of the play. Why is Scout narrating the story as an adult, rather than as a child?

Introducing the Characters

Writers use direct and indirect methods to reveal their characters. Good writers tend to rely on indirect methods of character development. It is far more effective to learn about characters by watching them in action than it is to be told what they are like. When good writers choose to comment on their characters' personalities, they often do so through the eyes of other characters who will see things from their own limited **perspectives**.

Major Characters in *To Kill a Mockingbird*

Bob Ewell
Tom's accuser is known in Maycomb as a local disgrace.

Atticus Finch
Scout and Jem's father is a prominent lawyer and the moral voice of reason in the novel.

Jean Louise "Scout" Finch
Atticus's daughter is a feisty tomboy and the narrator of the novel.

Most novels, such as *To Kill a Mockingbird,* have a protagonist and an antagonist. The protagonist is the central character. He or she must resolve a conflict over the course of the story, and often develop as a character as a result of facing this conflict. The protagonist of *To Kill a Mockingbird*, Atticus Finch, faces the challenge of defending an African American man wrongly accused of a heinous crime. By upholding the law, Atticus tries to help his children grow up without **prejudice**.

The antagonist is the character who stands in opposition to the protagonist. In some cases, he or she creates or represents the conflict that the protagonist has to overcome. Bob Ewell, the antagonist of the novel, accuses Tom Robinson of attacking his daughter, treats his family poorly, and threatens Atticus.

There are many different types of minor characters that assist in moving the plot forward. A dynamic character, such as Dill Harris, changes throughout the story, usually after facing conflict. A static character, such as Calpurnia, does not undergo changes. A flat character, such as Stephanie Crawford, has only one distinguishing personality trait, while a rounded character, such as Maudie Atkinson, has a more complex personality.

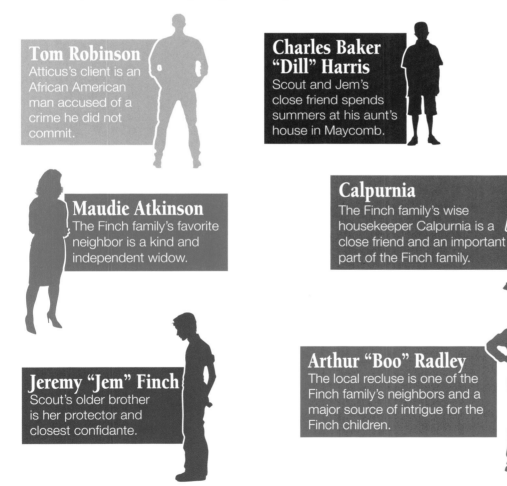

Tom Robinson
Atticus's client is an African American man accused of a crime he did not commit.

Charles Baker "Dill" Harris
Scout and Jem's close friend spends summers at his aunt's house in Maycomb.

Maudie Atkinson
The Finch family's favorite neighbor is a kind and independent widow.

Calpurnia
The Finch family's wise housekeeper Calpurnia is a close friend and an important part of the Finch family.

Jeremy "Jem" Finch
Scout's older brother is her protector and closest confidante.

Arthur "Boo" Radley
The local recluse is one of the Finch family's neighbors and a major source of intrigue for the Finch children.

Creating a Literary Device Analysis Booklet

Students will analyze the author's use of a literary device in the novel, and create a booklet to present this analysis. An exemplary literary device analysis booklet will meet the following criteria.

• Defines the chosen literary device accurately and in detail

• Places the definition of the literary device at the beginning of the booklet

• Provides strong, specific examples of how this literary device is used in the novel

• Describes examples in detail, with quotations properly integrated

• Includes thorough analysis of the use, purpose, and effectiveness of each example of how the chosen literary device is used in the novel

• Arranges all pages logically

• Examples are organized chronologically

• Provides no more than one example and its analysis per page

• Creates a neat, well-organized, and attractive booklet

• Booklet is colorful and displays the student's creativity

• Uses illustrations to represent the chosen literary device and the examples of how it is used in the novel

The Art of Storytelling

Storytelling is a way to entertain, engage with others, teach, or communicate perspectives on society. A narrative, or story, is a series of events that is often logically arranged. When writing his or her story, the writer structures the narrative in a particular way. The writer can also use different types of literary devices to create a distinct style and convey the narrative's overall message. In order to tell her story effectively, Harper Lee structured her narrative, created a plot, and used a number of literary devices in *To Kill a Mockingbird*.

Structure of a Narrative

Each narrative has a structure, which writers keep in mind when creating a story. The most common narrative structure, known as dramatic structure or Freytag's Pyramid, consists of five main components, which are all used in *To Kill a Mockingbird*.

Freytag's Pyramid

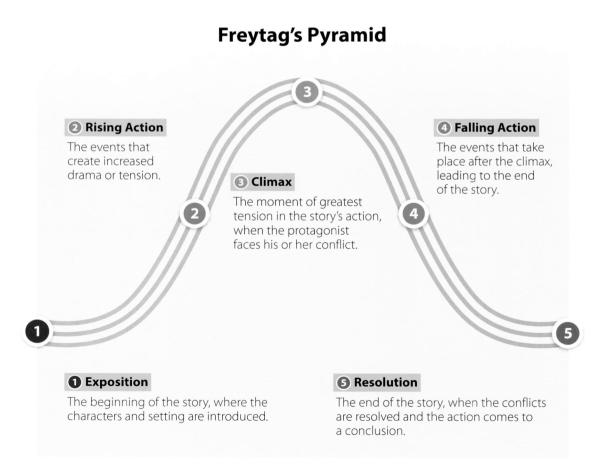

2 Rising Action
The events that create increased drama or tension.

3 Climax
The moment of greatest tension in the story's action, when the protagonist faces his or her conflict.

4 Falling Action
The events that take place after the climax, leading to the end of the story.

1 Exposition
The beginning of the story, where the characters and setting are introduced.

5 Resolution
The end of the story, when the conflicts are resolved and the action comes to a conclusion.

Plot

Every narrative needs to have a plot. Plot is the series of actions that propel the story forward. The plotline is the order in which events, or plot points, take place. These events build on each other and are organized in a logical manner. Each event causes the next event to happen, thus creating the narrative.

Plot Points in Chapter 3 of *To Kill a Mockingbird*

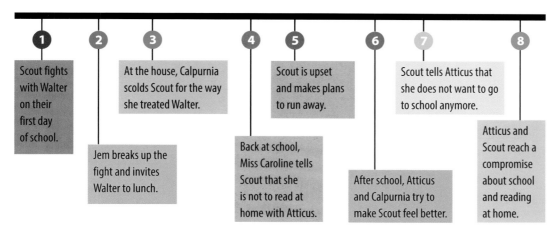

1 Scout fights with Walter on their first day of school.

2 Jem breaks up the fight and invites Walter to lunch.

3 At the house, Calpurnia scolds Scout for the way she treated Walter.

4 Back at school, Miss Caroline tells Scout that she is not to read at home with Atticus.

5 Scout is upset and makes plans to run away.

6 After school, Atticus and Calpurnia try to make Scout feel better.

7 Scout tells Atticus that she does not want to go to school anymore.

8 Atticus and Scout reach a compromise about school and reading at home.

Literary Devices

A literary device is any particular feature of a work of literature that can be identified, studied, and analyzed. There are two types of literary devices; they are literary elements and literary techniques.

Literary Elements

A literary element is a feature of a narrative that appears in almost every work of literature. The narrative needs these major features in order to be effective and engaging.

Action — Everything that occurs in a narrative.

Mood — The overall feeling that the narrative is intended to evoke within the reader.

Moral — The lesson that is intended to be taught through the narrative.

Literary Techniques

Literary techniques are the various ways a writer can manipulate language to convey meaning or to create a distinct style.

Personification — The attribution of human traits to something that is not human to give it a more vibrant description.

Satire — The use of humor and exaggeration to comment on the ridiculousness of something and make a point about it.

Allusion — A reference made to something the reader is presumed to know. An allusion can refer to a work of literature, history, or pop culture.

TEACHER NOTES

▶ **Video**

A Remembrance of Harper Lee
Draw conclusions as to why Harper Lee was a significant and celebrated storyteller.

1. What do you consider to be Harper Lee's legacy? Why will her novel matter in the future?
2. Harper Lee famously lived a quiet, private life, and gave her last interview in 1964. If you could ask Lee a question about her life and work, what would you ask? What would you like to know about her?

🧠 **More**

Examples of Literary Devices from the Novel
Recognize and understand the significance of various literary devices and explain their appeal. Analyze how Harper Lee's choices concerning literary devices contributed to the overall narrative.

1. Choose a literary device and analyze its use in the novel.
2. How does Lee use this literary device in the novel? Cite specific examples.
3. What is Lee's purpose when using this literary device? Is it effective?

Theme in the Novel

T he theme of a story is the underlying topic, idea, or position. It is often a general, **universal** statement about life. Sometimes, the theme is clearly stated, and other times it is suggested.

A theme is different from the topic of a novel. While a topic is the overall subject of a novel, a theme makes a statement about the topic in question. Theme can be expressed through the events that take place in the story, the ideas repeated along the way, and the lessons characters learn. The theme of a story is often open to interpretation. A reader may have to examine many different aspects of the novel in order to form an opinion about the story's theme.

Values

Closely related to the novel's themes are the **values** held by the novel's characters. In any novel, different characters uphold different values. These values are revealed through the words and actions of the characters. In some cases, a character's values will reflect those of the novel's writer. Sometimes, these values will inform or become the basis of a particular theme in the novel.

Major Themes of *To Kill a Mockingbird*

Not only does *To Kill a Mockingbird* entertain the reader with an engaging and moving narrative, it also acts as a social commentary. The novel illustrates the universal challenges of growing up and learning about the harsh realities of the world. Additionally, the novel includes themes of morality, social inequality, and prejudice.

Atticus Finch

Morality

"If you can learn a simple trick, Scout, you'll get along a lot better with all kinds of folks. You never really understand a person until you consider things from his point of view … until you climb into his skin and walk around in it."

Atticus Finch, Chapter 3

Jem Finch

Social Inequality

"I've thought about it a lot lately and I've got it figured out. There's four kinds of folks in the world. There's the ordinary kind like us and the neighbors, there's the kind like the Cunninghams out in the woods, the kind like the Ewells down at the dump, and the Negroes … The thing about it is, our kind of folk don't like the Cunninghams, the Cunninghams don't like the Ewells, and the Ewells hate and despise the colored folk."

Jem Finch, Chapter 23

Atticus Finch

Prejudice

"Those are twelve reasonable men in everyday life, Tom's jury, but you saw something come between them and reason. You saw the same thing that night in front of the jail … There's something in our world that makes men lose their heads—they couldn't be fair if they tried. In our courts, when it's a white man's word against a black man's, the white man always wins. They're ugly, but those are the facts of life."

Atticus Finch, Chapter 23

Secondary Themes

Secondary themes are those that are not heavily emphasized in the narrative. While it does not play as large a role as a major theme, a secondary theme adds another layer to the ideas presented by the novel, allowing for a more complex narrative and deeper literary analysis. Examples of secondary themes explored in *To Kill a Mockingbird* include **class**, courage, race, **justice**, fear, femininity, and family.

Creating a Symbolism Poster

Students will choose one of the other symbols listed on page 19 and analyze its role in the novel. They will then create a poster to present their analysis. An exemplary symbolism poster will meet the following criteria.

- Presents a clear purpose that is conveyed throughout the poster
- Shows an understanding of the concept of symbolism and the role it plays in the novel
- Provides an in-depth analysis of what the symbol represents
- Discusses the role the symbol plays in the novel
- Clearly indicates where the symbol appears in the novel
- Uses specific, detailed examples from the text to support the analysis
- Makes clear connections to the text
- Properly integrates all quotations
- Organizes the information in a logical, easy-to-read manner
- Includes high-quality graphics that relate to the symbol and effectively enhance understanding of the topic
- Features clear and concise writing
- Uses correct spelling, grammar, and punctuation
- Clearly labels items of importance
- Headings and subheadings are clear and easy to read
- Uses layout to creatively enhances the information
- Creates a poster that is attractive in terms of layout, design, and organization
- Shows a strong effort by the student

Symbolism in the Novel

Symbolism is a literary technique writers use to help convey theme. A symbol is often a tangible object, such as a mockingbird, to which a writer lends deeper meaning. Other times, action or dialogue in the narrative can be symbolic of a specific idea or theme.

Symbolism helps to give the novel's events, characters, and themes a universal feel. Sometimes, it sheds light on how the writer feels about specific concepts and ideas. When studying a work of literature, the reader can gain a deeper understanding of the story by identifying and analyzing the symbols used by the writer. If the reader has trouble identifying symbols in the novel, a good place to look first is the novel's title.

To Kill a Mockingbird

"Mockingbirds don't do one thing but make music for us to enjoy. They don't eat up people's gardens, don't nest in corncribs, they don't do one thing but sing their hearts out for us. That's why it's a sin to kill a mockingbird."

Maudie Atkinson, Chapter 10

The Mockingbird as a Symbol

The mockingbird can be interpreted as a symbol of innocence in the novel. The killing of a mockingbird would then symbolize of the destruction of innocence. While no actual mockingbird appears in the novel, the immorality of killing one is introduced when the Finch children receive their first air-rifles. Atticus knows Scout and Jem will want to shoot at birds, so he tells them it is a sin to kill a mockingbird, a fact that Maudie Atkinson confirms.

LAYING EGGS
The northern mockingbird **lays 3–4 eggs** per brood, on average.

WINGSPAN
A mockingbird's **wingspan** is around **10 inches**. (25 centimeters)

DEFENSE
Mockingbirds **fiercely defend** their nests, and often **attack cats** that come too close.

Who is the Mockingbird?

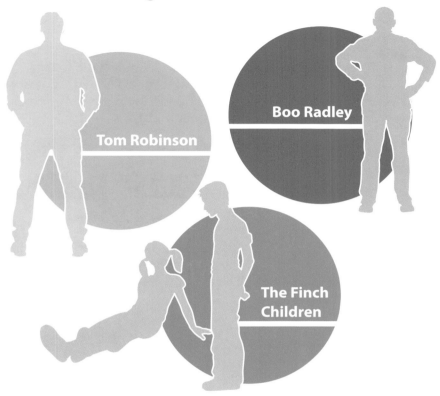

Other Symbols in the Novel

The Radley House

The Radley house is a symbol of the fear of the unknown. Like its reclusive inhabitant, the house is isolated from the community, and it becomes a place of mystery.

The Mad Dog

The mad dog is a symbol of the spread of fear that allows a community to go mad. The dog scares the people in the neighborhood, who worry he will spread rabies, and it is Atticus who has to shoot the dog.

Flowers

The prejudiced Mrs. Dubose is proud of the camellias in her garden. The stubborn nature of this flower represents her narrow-minded values and how difficult it is for others to change her mind. In contrast, Maudie Atkinson is fond of growing azaleas, which thrive in difficult conditions. This flower symbolizes her progressive attitude, as well as her independent spirit.

TEACHER NOTES

 Weblink

The Northern Mockingbird in the National Audubon Society Field Guide
Explore the National Audubon Society's Field Guide webpage on the northern mockingbird, including recordings of its unusual calls.

More

Extra Information on the Northern Mockingbird
Determine how the northern mockingbird's traits and history are related to the novel's events and themes.

1. How does the northern mockingbird itself relate to the novel? Use specific evidence.
2. Why do you think Harper Lee chose a mockingbird as the central symbol in the novel?

 More

Excerpts Illustrating How These Three Characters Can Be Seen As Mockingbirds
Recognize and understand the significance of symbolism and explain its appeal. Analyze how a specific symbol contributes to the novel's overall structure and meaning.

Choose one of the other symbols and answer these questions.

1. How does this symbol support Lee's purpose and perspective? Cite thorough textual evidence to support your analysis.
2. How is this symbol connected to the themes of the novel?
3. How does Lee's use of language and imagery support and enhance her use of this symbol?

Holding a Classroom Debate

Students will form groups and prepare arguments for a debate on a controversial issue. Exemplary performance in a debate will meet the following criteria.

- Demonstrates in-depth understanding of the topic and related information
- Presents strong, logical, and convincing arguments
- Communicates in a clear and confident manner
- Maintains eye contact
- Uses clear vocal tone and a reasonable rate of vocal delivery
- Uses respectful and appropriate language and body language
- Delivers arguments, evidence, and counter-evidence in an engaging and persuasive manner
- Supports each major point of an argument with several relevant and detailed facts and examples
- Connects all arguments to the overall topic in a clear, concise, and organized manner
- Presents the arguments and supporting evidence in a clear, logical manner
- Presents clear, thorough, and accurate information throughout the debate
- Addresses all of the opposing team's arguments with counter-arguments
- Identifies any weakness in the opposing team's arguments
- Constructs strong and relevant counter-arguments using accurate information
- Presents strong and persuasive arguments throughout the debate
- Summarizes the arguments in the closing statement

The Use of Language

Language is always evolving, with new words, phrases, and meanings coming into common use. Oxford Dictionaries updates its English dictionary quarterly, sometimes adding hundreds of new entries. These include slang terms and vocabulary based on current cultural trends. Here are some terms added to the Oxford English Dictionary in 2014 and 2015.

Idioms

An idiom is a commonly used expression with a meaning different from the literal definition. The meaning of an idiom is intended to be understood figuratively, and cannot always be deduced from the words used. When someone is learning a new language, idioms are often the most difficult aspect to understand. There are many idioms that are used in a particular geographic region, such as the Southern United States, the setting of *To Kill a Mockingbird*. Southern idioms are colorful and often make use of hyperbole.

Examples of Southern Idioms

If someone is acting frantic and confused, a Southerner might say they are **"runnin' like a chicken with its head cut off."**

To describe someone who is lazy, a Southerner might say, **"he's about as useful as a steering wheel on a mule."**

To describe someone who is annoying, a Southern might say, **"she could start an argument in an empty house."**

"I'll tan your hide" is a threat a Southerner may hear if they are in big trouble.

An idiom used in *To Kill a Mockingbird* is **"she had an acid tongue,"** meaning Miss Maudie speaks sharply. Another idiom used in the novel is **"Jem walked on eggs,"** meaning he acted carefully.

Words and Phrases Used in *To Kill a Mockingbird*

As *To Kill a Mockingbird* is set in the 1930s, many of the words and phrases used in the novel are specific to the decade and are unfamiliar to younger generations. It is important to note that some language used in the 1930s is considered inappropriate today. Additionally, some language used today would have been seen as inappropriate in the 1930s. Throughout the United States, people use terms and expressions specific to their geographical region. Here are a number of words and phrases used in *To Kill a Mockingbird* that reflect the time and place in which the novel is set.

Creating a Podcast

Students will research a notable event that took place during the Civil Rights Movement and communicate their research and make connections to the novel by creating a podcast on this event. An exemplary podcast will meet the following criteria.

- Demonstrates thorough knowledge of the topic
- Demonstrates understanding of the purpose of creating a podcast
- Presents information with the target audience in mind
- Focuses on a specific, narrow topic
- Uses accurate, specific, high-quality facts and details in the podcast
- Organizes and presents the main points and supporting facts in a logical, effective manner
- Begins with an engaging introduction to grab the listener's attention
- Establishes a clear purpose to the podcast immediately
- Identifies the speaker, the location, and the date the podcast was produced
- Uses vocabulary that enhances the content of the podcast
- Uses correct grammar throughout the podcast
- Maintains focus on the main topic throughout the podcast
- Clearly summarizes the main information in the conclusion of the podcast
- Delivers the podcast in a well-rehearsed, conversational manner
- Enunciates clearly and with engaging rhythm and expression
- Edits the podcast to a length that will keep the listener engaged
- Uses audio effects to enhance the podcast
- Records it in a quiet environment free of background noises

Impact of the Novel at the Time of Publishing

When it was first published, *To Kill a Mockingbird* had a tremendous impact on American literature and society as a whole. The success of the novel also had an impact on its author, Harper Lee. Published in the early 1960s, *To Kill a Mockingbird*'s themes of prejudice and morality echoed many of the most pressing political and social issues of the time. The impact of the novel did not remain within the literary world. *To Kill a Mockingbird* influenced many other forms of art produced during this time.

PULITZER PRIZE

In 1961, Harper Lee won a Pulitzer Prize for *To Kill a Mockingbird*. Lee became the first author to win a Pulitzer for a first novel. After this win, *To Kill a Mockingbird* became and remains a staple in high school and middle school English language arts education.

Critical Acclaim

To Kill a Mockingbird became an immediate success when it was published in 1960. Critics praised the novel's gentle narrative style and rich characters. Lee later admitted that the success of the novel was overwhelming. This is often thought to be the reason why she was not a more prolific writer.

Social Impact

In his 1964 book *Why We Can't Wait*, civil rights activist Reverend Martin Luther King, Jr. references Atticus Finch as a symbol of nonviolent heroism. *To Kill a Mockingbird* was published in the throes of the Civil Rights Movement in the United States. At this time, African Americans fought against discriminatory laws and perceptions. The novel's abrogation of racial intolerance had a positive impact on the civil rights movement.

Generating Discussions

To Kill a Mockingbird has been credited as one of the most influential books in history. When it was published, it helped to encourage discussion about tensions between African Americans and citizens of European descent. Written during the Civil Rights Movement, Harper Lee's novel provided an opportunity for people to discuss some of the most pressing issues of the early 1960s.

TEACHER NOTES

👁 First Hand

Excerpt from *Why We Can't Wait* by Martin Luther King, Jr.
Cite strong and thorough textual evidence in the novel to support Martin Luther King, Jr.'s statement that Atticus Finch is a model of nonviolent heroism.

1. Analyze how King's word choice and structure support and develop his argument in this excerpt.
2. In referencing Atticus Finch, how does Martin Luther King, Jr. strengthen his argument?
3. How is King similar to Atticus?

📖 Document

One-Taxi Town: Fiction Reviews from *The New York Times*
Assess the opinions stated in one of the first literary reviews of the novel.

1. How does the writer present and support his statements about the novel?
2. Do you agree with the literary critic's opinions of the novel?
3. Write your own review of the novel. What would you like people who have not read the novel to know about it? What features of the novel do you consider to be the most important to cover?

Film Adaptation

Just two years after *To Kill a Mockingbird* was published, a film of the same name was released in theaters. The film won three Academy Awards, including Best Actor in a Leading Role, which Gregory Peck took home for his portrayal of Atticus Finch.

The most beloved and widely read Pulitzer Prize Winner now comes vividly alive on the screen!

To kill a Mockingbird starring GREGORY PECK

with MARY BADHAM · PHILLIP ALFORD · JOHN MEGNA · RUTH WHITE · PAUL FIX
BROCK PETERS · FRANK OVERTON · ROSEMARY MURPHY · COLLIN WILCOX

Impact of the Novel Now

Although first published more than 50 years ago, *To Kill a Mockingbird* continues to have a notable effect on the world. The novel is a staple in classrooms throughout the United States, and its messages about justice and racial inequality resonate with readers to this day. Although Harper Lee stayed out of the spotlight, the ongoing success and impact of *To Kill a Mockingbird* has solidified the novel as one of the most important pieces of American literature.

Since its original publication, *To Kill a Mockingbird* has **sold** more than **40 million copies** around the world.

To Kill a Mockingbird has been **translated** into more than **40 languages**.

To Kill a Mockingbird has been on *USA Today's* bestseller list for more than **900 weeks and counting**.

Monroeville Play

The Monroe County Museum in Monroeville, Alabama, has a dedicated Harper Lee exhibit. Since 1991, the museum has staged an annual production of *To Kill a Mockingbird*. Much of the performance is set inside Monroeville's old courthouse. After a licensing dispute in 2015, Harper Lee started a nonprofit company in order to allow the performance to continue each year.

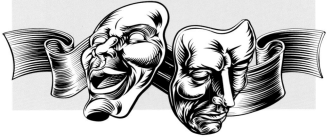

Treasured Film

The 1962 film *To Kill a Mockingbird* continues to be a highly influential film. The American Film Institute (AFI) has listed it as the 25th best American film, and as the greatest courtroom drama of all time. The AFI also ranked Atticus Finch as the greatest movie hero of all time. In 1995, the film was inducted into the National Film Registry of the Library of Congress.

Presidential Medal

In 2007, Harper Lee received the Presidential Medal of Freedom for her contribution to literature. First established in 1945, the Presidential Medal of Freedom recognizes people who have made "an especially meritorious contribution to the security or national interests of the United States, world peace, cultural or other significant public or private endeavors." The medal is the highest American honor that a civilian can receive.

SECOND NOVEL

In 2015, the novel *Go Set a Watchman* was published. Based on the first manuscript submitted by Harper Lee to her publishers, *Go Set a Watchman* is set 20 years after the resolution of *To Kill a Mockingbird*. Although its publication was controversial, both in the circumstances of its release and its depictions of characters, *Go Set a Watchman* sold more than 1.1 million copies during its first week of sales.

📄 Document

Harper Lee and the Presidential Medal of Freedom
Interpret the claims made by former U.S. President George W. Bush about Harper Lee's contribution to the culture and society of the United States.

1. After reading Bush's description of the Presidential Medal of Freedom, explain how Harper Lee "earned the respect of the American people." Why does she hold "a unique place in the story of our time"?
2. How does Bush's description of *To Kill a Mockingbird* reflect American values?

🌐 Weblink

Harper Lee Starts Non-Profit to Keep *To Kill a Mockingbird* Play in Monroeville
Determine why Harper Lee started a non-profit company to fund the annual Monroeville performance of *To Kill a Mockingbird*.

1. The annual Monroeville production stages the second act of the play inside Monroe County's Old Courthouse Museum. Why do you think they choose to stage it there?
2. If you were directing a production of *To Kill a Mockingbird*, how would you want the audience to feel at the end of the performance?

EXTENSION ACTIVITY

Creating a Timeline

Students will explore a topic related to the novel and create a timeline to present their research on historical events connected to this topic. An exemplary timeline will meet the following criteria.

- Includes the most significant events pertaining to the topic to be compared and analyzed
- Includes interesting events
- Uses accurate information for all events, including date, location, and major details
- Orders the events in a chronological sequence
- Describes each event with accurate, vivid, and specific details
- Presents the topic from three or more perspectives
- Inspires the reader to ask thoughtful questions regarding the events and perspectives presented in the timeline
- Uses correct spelling, grammar, and punctuation
- Presents the timeline in a visually attractive and striking manner
- Presents the timeline in a neat, organized manner that is logical and easy to follow
- Uses creativity to present the timeline in an engaging manner
- Effectively communicates the historical information relating to the topic
- Supports each event with reliable sources
- Expresses a clear purpose for creating the timeline
- Enhances the reader's understanding of the topic
- Includes a correctly formatted bibliography of all sources used to create the timeline

Perspectives on Racism and Social Equality

To Kill a Mockingbird's strong message regarding **racism** and social equality is what has made it an enduring novel for readers all over the world. By opposing the prejudice and inequality of the 1930s, Harper Lee's novel inspired readers who faced similar issues during their own time. The 1960s was a turbulent time in U.S. history, a decade characterized by major protests and victories for social equality.

African American History Timeline

1821 Thomas L. Jennings becomes the first African American to hold a patent.

1917–1935 An artistic and cultural explosion of African American talent, known as the Harlem Renaissance, takes place in Harlem, New York.

Notable Achievements

1800s **1900s**

Major Protests and Victories for Social Equality

1917 Racially motivated riots break out in East St. Louis, Illinois, where Caucasian resentment toward African Americans working in wartime industries led to violence.

1954 A court case known as Brown v. Board of Education results in the United States Supreme Court ruling that racial segregation in public schools is a violation of the Fourteenth Amendment.

1955 The Montgomery Bus Boycott starts after Rosa Parks is arrested for refusing to give up her bus seat to a Caucasian passenger in Montgomery, Alabama.

While many achievements have improved tensions between African Americans and Americans of European descent, many Americans say there is more to be done. "What we also have to remember is that the barriers that exist for them [young people of minorities] to pursue their dreams are deep and structural," said United States President Barack Obama in an interview with *Time* magazine in 2016. "We can do a lot to make sure that we're enforcing our nondiscrimination laws. We can do a lot more to open up people's perspective about who belongs where."

Transparency— Timeline

Notable Achievements/Major Protests and Victories for Social Equality

Analyze the themes and events of *To Kill a Mockingbird* in different cultural, historical, and contemporary contexts.

1. How was racism and social equality viewed at the time in which the novel is set? How is this illustrated in the novel?
2. How might the era in which Harper Lee wrote *To Kill a Mockingbird* have influenced the themes of the novel? What social history, events, and commonly held beliefs influenced perspectives on racism and social equality in the early 1960s?
3. How might these views have shaped the way a reader in the early 1960s would interpret the novel?
4. What current events, changes in laws, new ideas, or political discussions might shape perspectives on racism and social equality today?
5. How might these current events and present perspectives affect the way a reader interprets the topic of racism and social inequality as depicted in the novel?

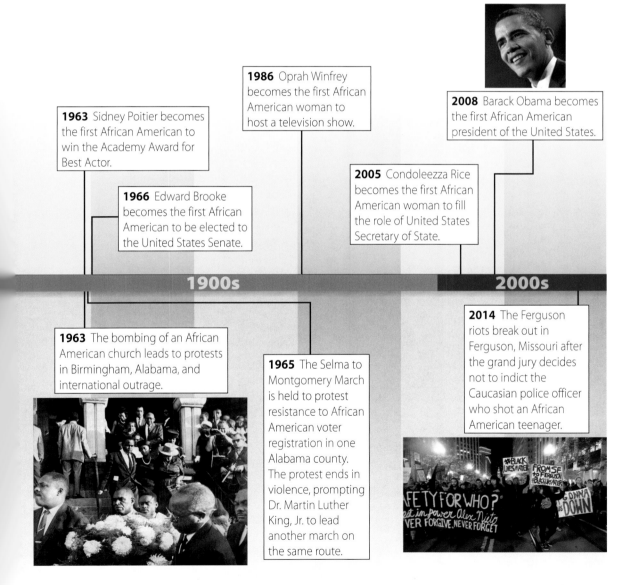

1963 Sidney Poitier becomes the first African American to win the Academy Award for Best Actor.

1986 Oprah Winfrey becomes the first African American woman to host a television show.

2008 Barack Obama becomes the first African American president of the United States.

1966 Edward Brooke becomes the first African American to be elected to the United States Senate.

2005 Condoleezza Rice becomes the first African American woman to fill the role of United States Secretary of State.

1900s

2000s

1963 The bombing of an African American church leads to protests in Birmingham, Alabama, and international outrage.

1965 The Selma to Montgomery March is held to protest resistance to African American voter registration in one Alabama county. The protest ends in violence, prompting Dr. Martin Luther King, Jr. to lead another march on the same route.

2014 The Ferguson riots break out in Ferguson, Missouri after the grand jury decides not to indict the Caucasian police officer who shot an African American teenager.

Writing a Comparative Essay

Students will compare two literary devices used in To Kill a Mockingbird, and then write a comparative essay based on their analysis. An exemplary comparative essay will meet the following criteria.

- Consists of a one-paragraph introduction, three body paragraphs, and a one-paragraph conclusion
- Introduction includes an engaging lead statement about the topic of the essay, more detailed information about the novel, and a one-sentence thesis that specifically states the essay's argument
- Body paragraphs include a topic sentence that refers to the thesis and how the idea appears in the novel, a supporting sentence that points to this part of the novel, textual evidence of this idea from the novel, and analysis of this evidence
- Body paragraphs end with a transition to the next paragraph
- Conclusion refers to the topic of the essay and the three points presented in the body paragraphs, and restates the thesis
- Provides a thorough analysis of the literary devices in question
- Cites strong and thorough textual evidence to support analysis of what the novel says explicitly
- Presents a clear, specific thesis that indicates a high level of critical engagement
- Organizes ideas in a logical manner
- Communicates arguments in a clear, effective manner
- Properly integrates all quotations
- Correctly cites all sources used
- Correctly formats bibliography

Writing a Comparative Essay

*T*o Kill a Mockingbird is brought to life with engaging characters, places, and themes. After studying the novel, write a comparative essay to explore how two literary devices are used in *To Kill a Mockingbird*. This could be a comparison of characters, themes, symbols, or settings. To write a comparative essay, you will need to formulate an argument. Your argument should clearly state how you feel your compared elements are similar or different. Support your argument with sufficient evidence from the novel and valid reasoning.

How to Analyze and Compare Characters

Use the chart to guide your comparison of two characters in *To Kill a Mockingbird*.

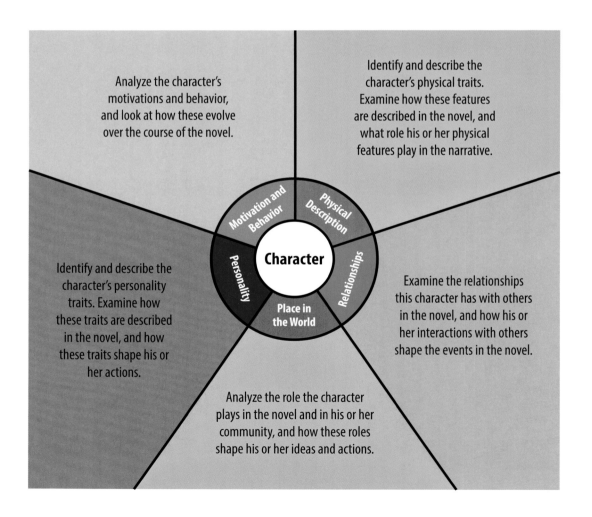

Comparing Atticus Finch and Bob Ewell

Atticus Finch

Personality
- Brave
- Fair
- Patient
- Empathetic
- Kind
- Described by other characters as a gentleman

Motivation and Behavior
- Lives by his code of ethics
- Works to always do the right thing and treat people fairly
- Wants his children to be respectful and kind
- Responds to conflict calmly and does not give in to violence

Place in the World
- The protagonist in the novel
- The moral role model in the novel
- Plays a respected role in his community as a lawyer
- Feels a responsibility to help those less fortunate than him

Relationships
- A widower
- Father of two young children
- Treats others with empathy and respect
- He has many friends
- His behavior is a good example for his children

Physical Description
- Middle aged
- Wears glasses
- Always wears a suit
- Uses language that indicates he is educated

Place in the World
- The antagonist in the novel
- He has a low social standing in Maycomb
- Known for being rough and uneducated
- Represents prejudice and evil in society

Physical Description
- Looks as if he does not bathe
- Small in stature
- Red-faced
- Uses language that indicates he is uneducated

Motivation and Behavior
- Motivated by his prejudice against African Americans
- Acts on anger and embarrassment
- Wants revenge on people in Maycomb
- Responds to conflict through violence

Relationships
- A widower
- Father of eight children
- Treats his children badly
- Interacts with others in a blunt manner
- Treats others with contempt and hatred

Personality
- Coarse
- Unkind
- Angry
- Lazy
- Narrow-minded
- Vengeful

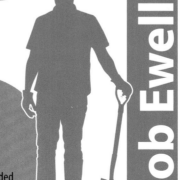

Bob Ewell

TEACHER NOTES

Transparency– Chart

Questions for Character Analysis

Analyze how specific character features, such as conflicts, motivations, relationships, and influences, affect the plot of *To Kill a Mockingbird*. Cite strong and thorough textual evidence to support analysis of what the novel says explicitly as well as inferences drawn from the novel.

Quiz Answers
1. A
2. B
3. D
4. A
5. C
6. B
7. C
8. B
9. A
10. D

Key Words

class: divisions in society based on economic, cultural, or political features; these divisions determine an individual or group's social rank

justice: fair, moral behavior or treatment; the administration of laws to fairly and objectively judge those accused of crimes

morality: a belief system based on principles of what is right and wrong, and using this system to make decisions based on ethics and doing the right thing

prejudice: a preconceived opinion or idea formed without reason or sufficient knowledge

perspectives: a certain point of view or position regarding a subject

racism: intolerance of a racial group, often based on the idea that one particular racial group is superior to others

segregation: the act of separating specific groups, often based on race, class, or religion, from the rest of society; this can be done in restricting the use of particular places to certain groups

social inequality: a lack of equality in regards to one's rank within society

universal: common to all cases; present or appearing in all conditions

values: an individual's standards of behavior and what aspects of life they consider to be most important

Literary Terms

action: everything that occurs in a narrative

antagonist: the character who stands in opposition to the protagonist; in some cases, the antagonist creates or represents the conflict that the protagonist faces

bibliography: a list of sources used in a written work

climax: the moment of greatest tension in the story's action

conflict: a struggle between two or more opposing forces, creating a tension that must be resolved

dialogue: the spoken conversations that the characters have with each other

exposition: the beginning of the story, where the characters and setting are introduced

falling action: the events that take place after the climax, leading up to the end of the story

Freytag's Pyramid: a narrative structure consisting of five elements; this includes exposition, rising action, climax, falling action, and resolution

hyperbole: exaggeration used for emphasis

idiom: a commonly used expression with a meaning that differs from its literal meaning

mood: the overall feeling that the narrative is intended to evoke within the reader

narrative: a logically arranged series of events presented for an audience; a story

narrator: the character or person telling the story, providing background information and opinions on the events, and connecting the gaps between major events and dialogue

plot: the specific action that propels a story forward

protagonist: the central character in a piece of fiction who must deal with a conflict and often undergoes some type of change as a result

resolution: the end of the story, when the problems are resolved and the action comes to a conclusion

rising action: the events that create increased drama or tension

style: the unique way that writers use language to tell their story; this can include word choice, the use of imagery, and the length and organization of sentences

symbolism: a stylistic device using symbols to represent and intensify concepts and ideas

theme: the underlying topic, idea, or position in a work that is often a general, universal statement about life

Index

LIGHTB◆X

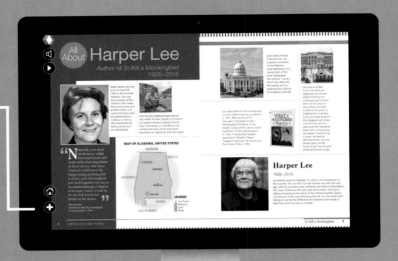

➕ SUPPLEMENTARY RESOURCES

Click on the plus icon ➕ found in the bottom left corner of each spread to open additional teacher resources.

- Download and print the book's quizzes and activities
- Access curriculum correlations
- Explore additional web applications that enhance the Lightbox experience

LIGHTBOX DIGITAL TITLES
Packed full of integrated media

VIDEOS
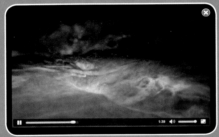

INTERACTIVE MAPS
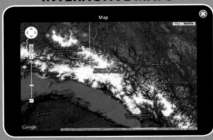

WEBLINKS

SLIDESHOWS

QUIZZES

OPTIMIZED FOR
✓ **TABLETS**
✓ **WHITEBOARDS**
✓ **COMPUTERS**
✓ **AND MUCH MORE!**

Published by Smartbook Media Inc.
350 5th Avenue, 59th Floor New York, NY 10118
Website: www.openlightbox.com

Library of Congress Control Number: 2016937396

ISBN 978-1-5105-1178-1 (hardcover)
ISBN 978-1-5105-1179-8 (multi-user eBook)

Printed in Brainerd, Minnesota, United States
1 2 3 4 5 6 7 8 9 0 20 19 18 17 16

072016
150716

Project Coordinator: Jared Siemens
Art Director: Terry Paulhus

Every reasonable effort has been made to trace ownership and to obtain permission to reprint copyright material. The publisher would be pleased to have any errors or omissions brought to its attention so that they may be corrected in subsequent printings. The publisher acknowledges Getty Images, Alamy, Corbis, Newscom, and iStock as its primary image suppliers for this title.